HENRY V

Retold by Robert Swindells

Illustrated by Mark Oldroyd

A & C Black • London

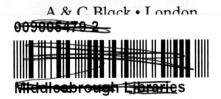

First published 2010 by
A & C Black Publishers Ltd
36 Soho Square, London, W1D 3QY

www.acblack.com

Text copyright © 2010 Robert Swindells
Illustrations copyright © 2010 Mark Oldroyd

The rights of Robert Swindells and Mark Oldroyd to be
identified as author and illustrator of this work respectively
have been asserted by them in accordance with the
Copyrights, Designs and Patents Act 1988.

ISBN 978-1-4081-2396-6

A CIP catalogue for this book is available from the British Library.

This book is produced using paper that is made from wood grown
in managed, sustainable forests. It is natural, renewable and
recyclable. The logging and manufacturing processes conform
to the environmental regulations of the country of origin.

Printed and bound in Great Britain
by CPI Cox & Wyman, Reading, RG1 8EX.

Contents

List of characters

Henry the fifth, *King of England*

Duke of Bedford, *brother to the king*

Duke of Gloucester, *brother to the king*

Duke of Exeter, *uncle to the king*

Duke of Westmoreland, *cousin to the king*

Duke of York

Earl of Salisbury

Earl of Warwick

Archbishop of Canterbury

Bishop of Ely

Earl of Cambridge, *conspirator against the king*

Lord Scroop, *conspirator against the king*

Sir Thomas Gray, *conspirator against the king*

Fluellen, *officer in the king's army*

Macmorris, *officer in the king's army*

Gower, *officer in the king's army*

Sir Thomas Erpingham, *officer in the king's army*

Bardolph, *soldier in the king's army*

Nym, *soldier in the king's army*

Pistol, *soldier in the king's army*

Bates, *soldier in the king's army*

Court, *soldier in the king's army*

Williams, *soldier in the king's army*

Boy

Charles the sixth, *King of France*

Lewis, *the dauphin*

The Constable of France

Duke of Britaine

Duke of Orleans

Grandpre, *a French lord*

Governor of Harfleur

Montjoy, *a herald*

Ambassadors to the King of France

Le Fer, *French prisoner*

Katherine, *daughter to Charles*

Alice, *her maid*

Nell Quickly, *married to Pistol*

Act One

Imagine kings and soldiers, rogues and lovers
Compressed like microcircuits 'twixt these covers.
Here too are seas, and battlefields and horses:
The serried ranks of two opposing forces.
Now, having scanned the pages of our book,
To view the action, close your eyes and look.

One day, during the reign of King Henry the fifth, two worried men were talking in a side room at the king's palace. One was the Archbishop of Canterbury, his companion, the Bishop of Ely.

'Listen,' growled the archbishop, 'there's talk of reviving that confounded Bill aimed at stripping the Church of half its wealth.'

Ely looked at him. 'What Bill, my lord? When *was* this?'

The archbishop spoke impatiently. 'Surely you remember – during the last king's reign. Luckily, those were troubled times and his late Majesty had more urgent things to think about. Now the blessed thing's back to haunt us.'

Ely pulled a face. 'So how might we resist it, my lord?'

The archbishop shook his head. 'I don't know, Ely, but resist it we must: the Bill would ruin us.'

'Will the king support us, d'you think?'

'Well,' said the archbishop, 'he's a good Christian and a level-headed monarch.'

Ely nodded. 'And he seems to love the Church.'

His companion smiled. 'Never thought we'd be saying *that* about him, Ely. Was he a wild youth or what?'

'I'll say,' chuckled Ely. 'I remember him in *Henry the Fourth – both* parts.' He grinned, then looked grave. 'But the Bill – is his Majesty for or against?'

The archbishop frowned. 'Well, Ely, the king's thinking of pressing certain claims in France that might lead to fighting, and fighting costs money, and I made him an offer – the biggest advance of Church money ever made to a king.'

'And how did he react?' asked Ely, eagerly.

The archbishop sighed. 'I *think* it swayed him towards us, but we were interrupted…'

'Interrupted?'

'Yes. The French ambassador chose that moment to request an audience with His Majesty. Is it four o'clock?'

'It is, my lord.'

'The king is due, then. Let's go in and find out what he wants.' The archbishop smiled. 'Not that I haven't a pretty fair idea already.'

As the two churchmen made their way towards the Presence Chamber from one direction, the king and five nobles entered it from another.

The king looked around. 'Where's the archbishop?' he asked.

'Not here,' said his uncle, the Duke of Exeter.

'Then send for him, Uncle.'

The Duke of Westmoreland looked at Henry. 'Shall we have the French ambassadors in, too, my lord?'

The king shook his head. 'Not yet, cousin. I need the archbishop to clear up a couple of points for me first.' He smiled wryly. 'Having claimed dukedoms in France, I don't want to have it turn out I'm not entitled to them.'

As King Henry spoke, the two churchmen entered the chamber. The archbishop spoke a loyal greeting. The king thanked him and said, 'There's a law, known as the Salic Law, which some say bars me from claiming the throne of France. I'd appreciate your opinion on it, and I want you to bear in mind that what you tell me might well lead to war, with all its dreadful consequences. Therefore, I want you to speak plainly and refrain from putting a spin on your advice. I don't want to be responsible for the death or destitution of thousands of my innocent subjects, in pursuit of an unjust claim.'

'Your Majesty,' replied the archbishop, 'the territories covered by this Salic Law lie in Germany, not France. The French are trying to bamboozle you with legalistic nonsense.'

The king gazed at the churchman. 'So you're saying I have right on my side in the matter of this claim?'

The archbishop nodded. 'Certainly.' *And while you're busy fighting the French*, he thought, but didn't say, *you won't have time to bother with this Bill the Commons seem so keen to resurrect.* He went on: 'Remember your illustrious ancestors, Majesty – your great-grandfather; your great uncle the Black Prince, how fiercely *they* fought in France; their glorious victories. You are their heir – you sit on their throne.'

'Remind your people of these valiant heroes,' put in Ely. 'Do what *they* did – make England great again.'

The Dukes of Exeter and Westmoreland weighed in with the same enthusiasm.

The king held up his hand. 'Whoa, just a minute!' He looked at the eager faces of his supporters. 'It's all very well rushing off to fight in France, but remember what always happens here in England while our armies are abroad.'

'What?' asked a noble.

'The *Scots*,' said Henry. 'Whenever England is left undefended, the Scots take the opportunity to invade. And I'm not talking about border raiders here, I mean full-scale invasion.' He smiled grimly. 'Remember the old saying: *If that you will France win, then with Scotland first begin.*'

Thinking the king was wavering, the archbishop spoke. 'Bees, Majesty,' he said. 'Consider honeybees. They share a basic aim, that of building and protecting the hive, but they divide their forces in order to accomplish a variety of tasks. Some build, some forage, some are soldiers, some tend the young. We must imitate the bees, dividing our armies into attackers and defenders. A quarter of an English army is enough to defeat the French, and the other three quarters will certainly deter the Scots.'

This generated patriotic fervour all round, and the king cried, 'Call in the dauphin's messengers.'

The French ambassadors were ushered in.

'Right,' said Henry. 'Let's hear what the dauphin has to say – I understand it was he, and not your king, who sent you?'

The first ambassador stepped forward. 'Yes, that's right. May we speak plainly, your Majesty?'

'Of course you may, you're not in the presence of savages. Speak!'

'Very well. You have laid claim to certain dukedoms in our country. The dauphin knows something of your Majesty's past conduct, and wants you to understand that there's nothing in France that can be won by skill on the dance floor. You'll find you can't booze your way into a dukedom, nor win a throne at the gaming table. He's sent you this gift, which he hopes will do instead.'

The king looked at the Frenchman through narrowed eyes. 'What is it?'

'Tennis balls, my liege.'

'How kind of the dauphin,' spat Henry.

'We thank him for his gift, and you for your pains. You may tell him his picture of me is out of date, and that I'll be over there shortly to play a game that'll make him wish he'd kept his balls to himself.'

Gesturing to attendants, the king told them to give the messengers safe conduct. Then he turned to the nobles. 'Prepare my army,' he snapped. 'Begin today. Spare no expense, waste no time, and by God we'll teach this dauphin what it means to jest with us.'

As news spread of Henry's thirst for action against France, war fever gripped England. People of all ranks and stations put aside their everyday concerns in order to ready themselves for the struggle. The very air tingled with expectation.

When reports of England's mood reached France, there was a sense that the dauphin's insult to Henry had unleashed something unstoppable. The King of France and his

16

advisers, deeply worried, attempted to restore normal relations between the kingdoms, but it was too late. England's blood was up, and only the sight of French blood would cool King Henry's rage.

Among those flocking to the king's colours in London were three disreputable characters who had been boozing pals to Henry in his wild, irresponsible youth. Henry had since changed beyond recognition, but his former cronies had not. Their names were Bardolph, Nym and Pistol, and they were a worthless trio. By chance, Bardolph and Nym bumped into each other outside the Boar's Head Tavern in Eastcheap.

'What *you* doing here, Nym, you peasant?' cried Bardolph.

'Same as you, I shouldn't wonder,' retorted Nym. 'Joining the army to serve the king wot used to be our boozing-mate, till the crown made him all hoity-toity.'

Bardolph laughed. 'We'll serve the king, and we'll serve ourselves while we're at it, Nym. Think of the looting – the stores and equipment lying around, just asking to be pinched.'

'Not *pinched*, mate,' protested Nym. '*Liberated*. Us soldiers says *liberated*.' He leered. 'There'll be French wenches needs liberating as well, and don't forget stripping the dead.'

'Of *both* sides,' amended Bardolph.

Nym nodded. 'Boaf sides, goes wivout saying. So you better call me *Corporal* Nym, and you can be *Lootenant* Bardolph – how's that?'

'Perfick,' purred Bardolph. 'Hey, are you talking to whatsisface yet – Pistol?'

'Why shouldn't I be?' growled Nym.

'He pinched your girlfriend, didn't he – Nell Quickly? They got married.'

'I'm not bovvered. Not enough to stick one on him, anyway. Life's too short, innit? Mind you, I'm not saying I might not do him in one of these days while he's asleep, but that'll be down to rendezvous or whatsit – serendipity.'

'Talk of the devil,' chuckled Bardolph, 'here's the man himself, and his lady wife. Stay cool, Corporal Nym.'

As Pistol and Nell drew near, Nym eyeballed his former friend. 'How's it going, my old flower?'

'I'm *not* your old flower, airhead,' snarled Pistol.

'Mebbe not, but *she* is.' Nym nodded at Nell and drew his sword.

'*Don't!*' cried Bardolph. '*Either* of you. Put up your swords, we're all on the same side here.'

'Same side as *him*?' sneered Pistol. 'Why, I'd as soon be comrade to a *pig*; to a *toad*. I'd as soon march beside a foul, festering tunnel-dwarf as be on the same side as that loser.'

Bardolph brandished his rapier. 'I swear,' he roared, 'if *either* of you goes to strike a blow I'll run him through with this.'

At that moment, a boy came running up. 'Mine host, Pistol,' he cried, 'come quick. You too, mistress. It's my master, John Falstaff.

He's took ill. Very ill. In fact, I think he might die.' He noticed Bardolph's flushed face. 'Your cheeks'd do him for a hot-water bottle, if you shoved your head under his sheets.'

'Get lost!' cried Bardolph. 'Go on, boy, or I'll...'

'*I'll* come to poor John,' said Nell. 'He's never been the same since he ran into the king and Henry pretended not to know him, though they'd caroused together on many a merry night. It killed his heart. Follow soon, husband.'

The woman hurried away, and Bardolph resumed his efforts to heal the rift between Nym and Pistol. After more fratching, Pistol agreed to pay a gambling debt he owed Nym, and the pair shook hands. Only then did the three rogues set off to bid farewell to their dying friend.

———————

As Bardolph, Nym and Pistol stood at Falstaff's bedside, three other rogues were exercising the minds of some of the king's loyal nobles at

Southampton. Diplomacy having failed, the French had adopted a different tactic. Their agents had found three men who, in exchange for gold, would betray their king and asassinate him at Southampton as he prepared to embark with his army for France. But three loyal nobles – Exeter, Bedford and Westmorland – had uncovered the plot and met in a council chamber to discuss the treacherous trio.

'Have you seen 'em,' growled Westmoreland, 'acting the faithful followers for all their worth, like butter wouldn't melt in their mouths?'

'Don't worry,' spat Exeter. 'His Majesty's not easily fooled. Those three are history if they did but know it.'

The men under discussion were Richard, Earl of Cambridge, Henry, Lord Scroop of Masham and Sir Thomas Grey, a knight of Northumberland. As the nobles discussed them, trumpets sounded and the three traitors appeared in the company of the king, who was asking their opinion on the army he'd assembled.

'D'you think we've got the beating of the French with this force?' he inquired.

'Aye,' nodded Scroop. 'If every man does his best.'

'Oh, they'll do their best,' said Henry. 'I haven't recruited any man who isn't as keen on achieving victory as I am myself.'

'Your people love you,' fawned Cambridge.

Grey agreed. 'Even your father's former enemies rally to your cause, sire.'

'I'm thankful for it, sir knight. And I shan't forget to reward those who serve me faithfully.'

Grey smiled. 'Then every man will certainly strive to do so.'

Henry remembered something, and turned to his uncle, Exeter. 'That soldier who disrespected me yesterday, Uncle. He'd been drinking, and I think it was the drink talking. I want him pardoned and released.'

Scroop looked at the king. 'Is that wise, your Grace? I think you ought to punish him, or others might be tempted to follow his example.'

'Oh, let us yet be merciful!' said Henry.

'You may be merciful and punish, too,' put in Cambridge.

'Absolutely, sire,' said Grey. 'To spare the fellow's life after inflicting much pain on him is more mercy than he deserves.'

'Oh, come,' rejoined the king. 'Your concern for me makes you too hard on the poor wretch.' He shrugged. 'If we deal harshly with small offences such as this, how shall we punish *real* iniquities when they arise?' He smiled. 'Anyway, it's time to concentrate on our French causes. The three of you applied for commissions in my army, I believe?'

The traitors nodded. 'Well,' said the king, 'I have them here. Richard, Earl of Cambridge, here's yours. And yours, Lord Scroop of Masham. And this one, sir knight, Grey of Northumberland, is for you.' He gazed at the three men. 'Read them, and you'll know I know what you're worth.' He turned to speak to his uncle, then broke off and looked again at the traitors. 'What's the matter?' he asked. 'You've gone pale. Is it something I said, or something you've read in those papers?'

Cambridge gulped. 'I ... I confess my guilt,' he croaked, 'and beg you be merciful.'

'We beg mercy, too,' said Scroop and Grey together.

'You may recall,' said Henry, 'that I was inclined a short while ago to show mercy, and the three of you advised against it. I'm inclined now to heed your advice, and since your crime is that of high treason, you must die.'

As the three disgraced nobles were led away, the king addressed his lords. 'By exposing this plot, God has shown that He blesses our enterprise, which therefore cannot fail. Cheerly to sea, the signs of war advance; No King of England, if not King of France!'

Act Two

Some men, when called to arms, take up their station
Out of duty, love for monarch, pride in nation.
Though low-born, they hold their heads on high,
Ennobled by their readiness to die.
For many though, a darker, sadder story:
Some come for plunder, others for vain glory.

As King Henry prepared to embark his army at Southampton, Pistol, Nym and Bardolph made ready to leave London. Their old friend Falstaff had just died and the three rogues, together with Mistress Quickly and the boy, were discussing where he might be now. Was his soul in heaven, or in hell?

Nym thought this irrelevant. 'I think we ought to be making a move,' he said. 'The king'll sail for France any time now.'

'Right,' said Pistol. 'Let's go.' He turned to his wife, whom he was leaving in charge of the tavern. 'Kiss me goodbye,' he said, 'and see that you keep my property safe till I get back.

Don't trust anybody. Remember – no cards, no cheques. Cash only – that's the way to go.'

Having made their farewells to Mistress Quickly, the three rogues set out for Southampton with the boy, dreaming of plunder rather than glory on the battlefields of France.

Meanwhile, in his palace, the French king was addressing his nobles. Everybody could see he was a worried man.

'The English are coming,' he warned. 'We've had them on our soil in the past, and it was never a happy experience. We must fortify our towns, strengthen our garrisons. There are dangerous times ahead.'

The dauphin, who had insulted Henry with his gift of tennis balls, looked at his father. 'It's good policy always to be ready for war,' he said, 'even when no war threatens. So by all means look to our preparations, but let's not go over the top here: let's not panic.' He smiled. 'We should act as though we've learned that the English intend to organise a morris dance, or something.'

There were gasps among the nobles, but the young man scoffed. 'King Henry's a joke, I tell you. A flabby layabout. As long as he's on the throne, France has nothing to fear from England.'

The Constable of France shook his head. 'You underestimate him, young man. He may have behaved foolishly in his youth, but all that's behind him now. Ask the messengers you sent to his court – the ambassadors. They've seen him, and his advisers. *They* know it's not a fool we're dealing with.'

The dauphin shook his head. 'You're wrong, my lord high constable, but no matter. It's probably better to overestimate one's opponent than to underestimate him.'

The French king broke in. 'We believe King Henry is strong, and we'll prepare accordingly. Remember, he's descended from a line of monarchs who've haunted us down the years.'

A messenger approached. 'Ambassadors have come from Henry, King of England, sire. They ask to speak to your Majesty.'

'Bring them in.' The king turned to his counsellors. 'See how he pursues us already, my friends.'

The dauphin pulled a face. 'A coward will chase a fleeing foe. Turn on 'em, Father. Show 'em you're not to be messed with.'

King Henry's ambassador proved to be the Duke of Exeter. The French king looked at him. 'From our brother of England?'

Exeter nodded. 'From him, your Majesty, and he requires that you surrender to him that which is rightfully his: namely, the French Crown.' He held out a sheaf of papers. 'Look at this pedigree. It shows my king to be directly descended from Edward the third, who sat on the throne you occupy now only as a result of happy coincidence.'

The French king gazed at Exeter. 'And if I *don't* surrender my crown, what then?'

'Why *then*,' growled Exeter, 'your country and its people will suffer as never before. That's the whole of my message, unless the dauphin is here.' The duke smiled thinly. 'My king has *another* message for him.'

The French king nodded. 'I need time to think about what you have said. You'll have my answer tomorrow.'

'And the dauphin?' enquired the dauphin. 'What does your king send to *him*?'

'His scorn and defiance,' Exeter replied. 'Slight regard, contempt. He wishes the dauphin to know that unless he has a favourable reply from your king, he will make the dauphin most bitterly regret his mocking gift of tennis balls.'

The dauphin sneered. 'If Henry has a favourable answer from my king, it will be against the dauphin's will. The dauphin wants nothing more than to fight England, which is why he sent the balls.'

'Yes, and Henry'll make your Paris Louvre shake for it,' spat Exeter.

'Tomorrow,' interrupted the French king, 'Henry shall have my answer in full.'

'I'd better leave now,' replied Exeter, 'before he comes himself to see what's taking so long.'

The French king watched through troubled eyes as the ambassador bowed and withdrew.

The next day, King Henry had the French reply, and he didn't like it. The French king was offering Henry the hand in marriage of his daughter Katherine, with a few worthless dukedoms thrown in. No mention of the French Crown. The English army was drawn up near the town of Harfleur. Henry's response was to besiege the town and to launch an assault on it.

Harfleur was heavily fortified. A breach was made in its wall by cannon fire, but every time the English soldiers tried to get through it, they were beaten back. Seeing his troops beginning to lose heart, King Henry spurred his horse into their midst and, waving his sword, cried out to rally them.

'Once more unto the breach, dear friends, once more; or close the wall up with our English dead.'

It thrilled the soldiers to hear the king call them his friends. They regrouped, determined not to let him down.

Henry saw their revived determination and cried, 'Follow your spirit; and upon this charge cry, God for Harry, England and Saint George!'

As the English troops charged, roaring towards the breach, Nym and his disreputable friends fell in at the rear.

'On!' cried Bardolph. 'On on on, to the breach, to the breach!'

'Hang on,' gasped Nym, 'it looks a bit dodgy to me; a bit dangerous, and I've only got the one life. The whole thing's too tasty if you ask me, and that's the penultimate troof.'

'You can say that again,' growled Pistol. 'There's altogether too much blood for my liking, too much heroic sacrifice. Shed-loads of immortal fame and not enough immortality, and *that's* about as penultimate as you can get.'

'Wish I was in a London ale house,' moaned the boy. 'I'd swap fame and glory for a foaming pint and homeland security any time.'

A man approached, looking fierce. His name was Fluellen and he was Welsh. He roared at the four rogues. 'Shift your bums, you slackers, d'you want to live for ever, or what? Get into that breach, NOW!' He used the flat of his sword to drive them forward.

Pistol appealed to him. 'Leave it out, Taff. Stop yelling at us, quit shoving. Be a bit more whatsit – *quintessential*, OK?'

Ignoring the slackers' pleas, Fluellen shepherded them towards the action.

The boy watched them go. He was starting to have doubts about his three adult friends. Adult they might be, but they weren't men. In fact, the three together wouldn't amount to one real man. They were petty thieves, chancers and cowards, nothing more. He resolved to break with them once and for all.

Having driven the three slackers to their duty, Fluellen became involved in a dispute with a brother officer, an Irishman by the name of Macmorris. Their argument was about the proper way to wage war, but there were racial overtones. As the men fratched, news came that the French were requesting discussions with the English. The quarrel had to be suspended, but the two men parted on unfriendly terms.

King Henry and his retinue met the Governor of Harfleur at the city gates. The king was in no mood to mess about – he laid it on the line.

'This is the last chance you'll get to surrender,' he told the governor. 'Yield now, and I'll treat your citizens with mercy. Fight on, and my soldiers will destroy Harfleur and show no pity in dealing with your people. *I* shan't be able to control them. They'll rape your young women and spit your infants on pikes, while their mothers howl in vain. They'll put young men to the sword and dash out the brains of old men against your walls. What d'you say, Governor? Will you fight on and be responsible for your people's ghastly fate, or surrender and obtain mercy for them?'

The governor shook his head and sighed. 'We expected the dauphin,' he murmured. 'He was to ride to our rescue at the head of a great army. Now he says he's not ready to lift so great a siege. We have no option but to surrender.'

The English entered Harfleur in triumph, but winter was coming and many of the soldiers were sick. King Henry directed his uncle Exeter to occupy the city with part of the army, and to fortify it against the French. He would lead the rest of his soldiers back to Calais for rest and recuperation.

The loss of Harfleur was a crippling blow to French morale. Many now believed the English advance to be unstoppable; the enemy would lay waste to all of France and place King Henry on the throne.

At the palace, Princess Katherine prevailed upon Alice, an English-speaking maid, to begin teaching her the language ahead of Henry's arrival.

The French king was equally pessimistic. 'Henry's crossed the Somme already,' he fretted.

'Yes,' said the Constable of France, 'and if we don't take a stand, we might as well leave the country altogether and let the English barbarians have it.'

'If they come unopposed,' vowed the Duke of Britaine, 'I'll sell up and buy a muddy farm in their miserable country.'

'I don't understand it,' grumbled the constable. 'How can men who spend their lives tramping through mud in the rain and cold, existing on weak barley broth, be so spirited, while we, sun-tanned and full of nourishing wine, behave like total wimps? Let's, for goodness' sake, make an effort, not let 'em walk all over us like we're not here.'

The dauphin chipped in. 'Our women,' he

complained, 'say all the spirit has been bred out of Frenchmen. They mean to give themselves to the vigour of English youth, in order to re-stock France with bastard warriors.'

Britaine nodded. 'They say we should all enrol at English dancing schools, since our skill lies only in our heels, which we show while running away.'

Listening to all this, the French king rallied. 'Find my herald, Montjoy,' he commanded. 'I'll send a message, telling Henry he needn't think we're going to stand aside and let him take France just like that.' He turned to his nobles and ordered them to muster their troops and go out to face the English. 'Bar Harry England,' he roared, 'that sweeps through our land with pennons painted in the blood of Harfleur. Take him, and bring him in chains to Rouen.'

The constable nodded approval. '*Now* you show greatness, your Majesty.' He smiled. 'I'm only sorry Henry's army is so small, and so sick. Why, when he sees our army he'll fall over his feet in his haste to surrender.'

The mood of the French court was transformed. The nobles hurried away to gather their troops. The herald was dispatched to ask King Henry how large a ransom he would pay to be allowed to return to England.

Only the dauphin was disappointed. He'd wanted to lead an army, too, but his father ordered him to remain with him at Rouen.

The English army was now in Picardy. A bridge there had been hotly contested between the French and English armies, but the French had been driven off. Immediately after this action, Captains Gower and Fluellen met behind the line.

'Have you come from the bridge, Fluellen?' asked Gower.

'Aye,' said Fluellen, 'and I saw brave action there.'

'Is the Duke of Exeter safe?'

'He is, and he kept the bridge most valiantly.

He had gallant help, mind – an old lieutenant by the name of Pistol, who fought like Mark Antony.'

Gower shook his head. 'Never heard of him.'

At that moment, Pistol came into view, and Fluellen said, 'Look you, here's the man himself.'

Pistol approached Fluellen. 'Captain,' he panted, 'I need a favour. The Duke of Exeter rates you, yeah?'

Fluellen shrugged. 'I've been able to do things for him from time to time, and he's not a man who forgets.'

'Well, I've got this mate, see? Bardolph. He's a terrific soldier – dead loyal, only Lady Luck done the dirty on him.'

Fluellen nodded. 'Lady Luck's like that. A man never knows where he is with her.'

'The thing is,' said Pistol, 'my mate was caught liberating a few bits and bobs from a church and the duke – well, he's only gone and condemned him to *death*, hasn't he. And I was wondering – well, the duke'll listen to you, right? If you was to tell 'im what a diamond geezer old Bardolph actually is when he's *not* nicking stuff out of churches, he might…'

Fluellen held up a hand. 'Listen, let me tell you something.' He gazed at Pistol. 'If Bardolph was my *brother*, and he'd been caught robbing a church, I'd urge the duke to hang him. We can't have English soldiers going round stealing from churches, it reflects on the whole army.'

'Yes, well,' snarled Pistol, 'thanks for your help, you Welsh git.'

'Hang about,' growled Gower. 'I *recognise* this guy now. He's nothing but a dosser, a layabout and a slimy little thief.'

Fluellen looked confused. 'But … the bridge. He told me how he'd fought for the bridge, see?'

'Huh!' scoffed Gower. 'Guys like this Pistol, they go where there's a war, and watch and listen. They learn stuff by heart – what happened here, who did what there, the name of this or that commander,who died bravely at such-and-such a spot. Then they go back to London and claim they were there, in the thick of it, playing the hero.' He shook his head. 'You've got to watch them, Fluellen, or they'll take you for everything you've got.'

Fluellen nodded. 'He had me fooled, I don't mind admitting.'

A drumbeat sounded. 'The king's coming,' said Fluellen, 'so there's lucky, 'cause I need to talk to him.'

The two captains hurried away. Pistol stood forgotten in the road, watching them go.

The king greeted Fluellen, and asked him how many of the Duke of Exeter's men had fallen defending the bridge.

'I don't believe the duke lost a single man,' Fluellen replied, 'unless you count a guy who was caught robbing a church and is likely to be hanged. His name's Bardolph, perhaps your Majesty's heard of him? Ugly brute, face like a slapped arse.'

The king nodded. 'Let him be hanged, and anybody else caught thieving. All French civilians are to be treated with respect. Nothing of theirs is to be taken unless it is paid for. Kindness will win us their goodwill, and lead on to victory.'

At this point, the French herald, Montjoy, appeared. King Henry looked at him. 'What're *you* doing here, Herald?'

'I have a message from my king.'

'I'll hear it.'

'Very well, it goes like this. You think we're dead but we've only been sleeping. We could have wiped the floor with you at Harfleur, but we decided to let war and sickness weaken your army further before confronting you. The time is now. You are weak and far from home. You must offer France a ransom in return for safe passage, or see your troops cut down. This ransom will take account of the great expense you have caused us by rampaging through our land. For you to kneel at my king's feet will not be enough: you must compensate France in full with English gold.'

King Henry fixed the herald with a cold stare, and spoke. 'Take this reply to your king, Montjoy. Tell him he's right: I *have* lost a lot of men, and those who remain are weakened by sickness, so they're not much better, man for man, than French troops. Fit, one Englishman equals three Frenchmen any time. But there: it's not like me to boast, something in your French air makes me do it, I think. Anyway, tell your master we wouldn't choose to fight in our present condition, but we won't run away, either. There'll be no ransom. We'll advance, even if France *and* some allied nation stand in our path, and we'll soak your French earth with French blood if we must.'

Montjoy bowed. 'I will deliver as you have said, Highness.'

The herald departed, and the Duke of Gloucester growled, 'I hope they don't attack us now.'

King Henry looked at him. 'We're in God's hands, not theirs. March the men to the bridge. We'll make camp on the far bank, and press on tomorrow.'

The French army was nearby, camped near a village called Agincourt. A group of nobles took their ease in a tent and passed the time by boasting.

'I wish it were morning,' said the Lord High Constable of France. 'I've got the best armour in the world.'

The Duke of Orleans nodded. 'It's good, your armour, but what about my horse?'

'Best horse in Europe,' conceded the constable.

The dauphin looked at the pair. 'You talk about horses and armour?'

Orleans nodded. 'You're as well provided with both as any prince in the world.'

'What a long night this is,' sighed the dauphin. 'I wouldn't swap my horse for any steed on four legs. He's a Pegasus: a flying horse. He's my mistress, I've written poems to him.'

The constable smiled to himself. He saw through the dauphin: knew him for a vain and boastful youth, full of hot air. When the young man left the tent to prepare for battle, he and Orleans fell to quarrelling over him.

'The dauphin wants to eat the English,' said Orleans.

'I think he will eat all he kills,' growled the constable, meaning he didn't expect the youth to kill anybody.

'He's a gallant prince,' defended Orleans. 'He never did harm that I heard of.'

'No, and he'll do none tomorrow,' retorted the constable.

The pair bickered till a messenger appeared. 'My lord high constable,' said the messenger, 'the English lie within fifteen hundred paces of your tent.'

'What, has somebody been measuring?'

'The Lord Grandpre.'

'Good for him, and roll on day,' cried the constable. 'I bet poor Henry isn't impatient for morning. If his men had any idea what was coming to them, they'd run away.'

The messenger shook his head. 'The island of England breeds very valiant creatures: thier mastiffs are unmatchable for courage.'

'Stupid mutts that charge into the jaws of a Russian bear and get their skulls crushed,' growled Orleans. 'Might as well say a flea is valiant if it takes its breakfast on a lion's lip.' He smiled. 'It's two o'clock, but let me see – by ten, we shall have each a hundred Englishmen.'

Act Three

There's strength in numbers, so the adage goes:
The big battallions crush their lesser foes.
Remember though, in scorn or in despair,
   How David slew Goliath, how the tortoise beat
the hare.

The night dragged on, the armies lying so close to each other that soldiers glimpsed through smarting eyes the faces of their enemies caught momentarily by firelight. The slightest noise carried between the camps, and when a horse neighed, it was impossible to tell from which camp the sound arose.

The French, cockily secure in their superior numbers, joked or played at dice, waiting eagerly for morning.

King Henry, exhausted like his men, gave himself no rest. He knew his soldiers lay apprehensive in the dark, realising they were heavily outnumbered, half expecting the coming dawn to be their last. And so he toured the English camp, alone and on foot, calling them his friends, speaking soft words of cheer and encouragement: a little touch of Harry in the night.

Later, wishing to meditate alone, the king borrowed a cloak to conceal his identity, and walked unrecognised among the tents. Presently, he approached Pistol, who asked him who he was.

'A friend,' replied Henry.

'Hofficer, are you?' pressed Pistol. 'Or one of the peasants like me?'

'I am a gentleman of a company,' the king told him. 'And yourself – who are *you*?'

'As good a gentleman as the Emperor,' lied Pistol.

'Then you are better than the king,' chuckled Henry.

'He's all right, the king is,' said Pistol. 'One of the lads. I love him, and kiss his dirty shoes. What's your name, mate?'

'Harry le Roy.'

'Le Roy!' exclaimed Pistol. 'A Cornish name.

Cornish then, are you?'

'No, I'm Welsh.'

'So you'll know Fluellen?'

'Yes.'

'Well, you can tell him I'll stick his leek right in his earhole on Saint David's Day.'

The king laughed. 'I wouldn't wear my dagger in my cap that day if I were you – Fluellen might stick that in *your* earhole.'

'Why – are you his mate or sommink?'

'Yes, and his relative as well.'

'Nuts to you then, that's what I say.'

'Thanks. God be with you.'

'Name's Pistol.'

'Suits you.' And with that the king walked away, passing unrecognised close to Captain Fluellen, just as Captain Gower approached.

'Captain Fluellen!' cried Gower.

'Ssssh!' hissed the Welshman. 'The French camp's about three inches away, d'you want 'em knowing all our names?' He sighed. 'Look back at the history of warfare, Gower. Pompey the

Great. You'll find there wasn't a lot of rabbiting on in *his* camp. It's against the ceremony and the care and the sobriety and the modesty of warfare, look you.'

Gower pulled a rueful face. 'Sorry. The *French* are loud, though, I've been hearing 'em all night.'

Fluellen scoffed. 'So because the French are wittering airheads, it's all right for us to be wittering airheads, too – is *that* what you think?'

Gower shook his head. 'Of course not, I will speak lower.'

'See that you do.'

The king, who had overheard this exchange, nodded to himself. *Though it appears a little out of fashion*, he thought, *there is much care and valour in this Welshman.*

Three figures loomed in the dark: common soldiers named John Bates, Alexander Court and Michael Williams.

'Look,' said Court, 'isn't that the break of dawn?'

'I think so,' Bates replied. 'Not something *we* particlarly want to see though, is it?'

Williams shook his head. 'We're looking at the start of a day we might not see the end of.' He caught sight of the disguised king. 'Who goes there?'

'A friend,' said Henry.

Williams was suspicious. 'Who's your captain?'

'Sir Thomas Erpingham.'

The soldier nodded. 'One of the good ones, Sir Thomas. How does he reckon it'll go today?'

Henry shrugged. 'Badly.'

'And has he told the king this?'

'No,' said Henry, 'and it wouldn't be fair if he did. Deep down, a king's a man like any other. When there's reason to be afraid, he's afraid. Difference is, *he* can't speak his fear or show it, because it'd demoralise the men.'

'Know what?' said Bates. 'I bet that however brave he looks, and no matter what he says, King Henry's wishing he was standing up to his neck in the Thames right now, and *I* wish he *was*, with me at his side.'

'You're mistaken, friend,' retorted Henry warmly. 'I'm sure the king would rather be here than anywhere else today.'

'Then I wish he was here by himself,' growled Bates. 'So he could buy his life with a ransom and save a lot of poor men who won't get that option.'

Henry shook his head. 'I don't believe you think so little of King Henry that you *really* wish him here alone. I think you're quite prepared to die in his company, since he's got right on his side.'

'How do *we* know he's got right on his side?' queried Williams.

Bates shook his head. 'Don't matter, mate. We're the king's subjects, it's our duty to fight for him. If his cause be wrong, the crime's his. *We're* only obeying orders.'

'Aye,' retorted Williams. 'And that lays a heavy burden on the king's soul, doesn't it?

All those mutilated corpses, widows and children left to starve. All innocent, killed because they owed a duty to the king.' He looked at Henry. 'Killed *by* the king, you might as well say.'

'Oh, I'm not so sure about *that*,' disputed Henry. 'How do we know that those who die haven't done wrong *before* they were called to serve? Their death in battle may be retribution for a lifetime of wrongdoing. Are you saying that when the king takes a man into his army, he becomes guilty of any crime the man may have committed in the past?' He shook his head. 'Every subject's duty is the king's, but every subject's *soul* is his own.'

'I wouldn't expect the king to answer for *my* sins,' declared Bates. 'I'll fight like hell for him, whatever.'

Henry nodded. 'I heard the king say he won't be ransomed.'

'Aye,' said Williams, 'he *said* so to make us fight, but he might change his mind after our throats are cut, and us none the wiser.'

'If he did that,' retorted Henry, 'I'd never trust his word again.'

Williams scoffed. 'Yeah, like he'd lose a lot of sleep over *that*. A king don't give a toss what guys like us think, you sad plonker.'

'I resent your tone,' snapped Henry. 'I'd give you a good battering if we weren't about to fight on the same side.'

'*After*,' snarled Williams. 'We'll have it out after, if we live, right?'

'Fine by me,' grated Henry.

The soldier glared at him. 'How will I recognise you?'

'Give me your glove,' said Henry. 'I'll wear it in my cap, and if you've the bottle to challenge me, I'll make you regret it.'

'And I'll wear one of yours,' said Williams, 'and if you come up to me and say *that's my glove*, I'll stick it where the monkey stuck his nuts.'

Leaving the three soldiers, the king resumed his solitary meditations, and a short time later,

Sir Thomas Erpingham sought him out.

'My lord,' he said, 'your nobles have been looking all over the camp for you,'

'Get them together in my tent,' instructed Henry. 'I'll be there shortly.'

When Erpingham had gone, the king offered up prayers for victory, till the Duke of Gloucester came to escort him to his tent, where the nobles awaited him. It was nearly morning.

At the French camp, the nobles prepared their steeds for battle as the rising sun struck flashes off their armour. The knights were high, pumped up with confidence.

A messenger appeared. 'The English are mustered for the fight!' he cried.

'Mount up!' ordered the Constable of France. '*Look* at 'em, what a pathetic show. The *sight* of us will knock the stuffing out of 'em before we strike a blow. There aren't even enough of 'em to give us all a go – our peasants could mop 'em up by themselves, if honour didn't compel us to get in the act.' He laughed. 'Anyway, let's do our little bit and get it over.'

Grandpre now appeared. 'What're you hanging about for, my lords of France?' he bellowed. 'That's not an *army*, it's a heap of rubbish, and it's making the place look untidy. Spur your mounts, get down there and sweep it up.'

'The English have said their prayers,' joked the constable, 'now they're waiting to die.'

'Maybe we ought to send 'em dinners and fresh kit,' mocked the dauphin, 'and fodder for their nags, *then* fight 'em.'

'For goodness' sake, let's just get *on* with it,' said the constable, though it hardly seemed worth the effort.

In the English camp, the nobles were mounting their horses, wishing one another luck, taking leave of each other lest they shouldn't meet again in this life. None of them was defeatist, but they weren't fools, either. The French, with sixty thousand men, outnumbered the English five to one, and the French soldiers weren't tired as their opponents were.

The Duke of Westmoreland looked at the king. 'I wish we had ten thousand of the men in England who'll do no work today.'

'No, cousin.' Henry shook his head. 'If we die today, England will have lost enough men. And if we win, the fewer we are, the greater each man's share of the honour. In fact...' He gazed at his cousin. 'You may announce that any man who doesn't relish the coming fight may drop out and go home. I'll pay his fare and guarantee him safe passage – we wouldn't want to die in that man's company.' He looked at his nobles. 'Today is Saint Crispin's Day. Every Englishman who survives this battle will hold his head high whenever Crispin's Day comes round, and show his wounds, and say "these wounds I had on Crispin's Day". Old men forget, but from now on the very *name* Crispin will cause men to remember *us* with pride – we few, we happy few, we band of brothers. And gentlemen in England now abed shall think themselves accursed they were not here, and hold their manhoods cheap while any speaks that fought with us upon Saint Crispin's Day.'

The Earl of Salisbury came forward. 'My sovereign lord,' he cried. 'The French are about to charge.'

'We're ready,' said the king.

'Perish the man who's not,' growled Westmoreland.

Henry glanced at him. 'You don't want more help from England, then?'

His cousin shook his head. 'I don't. In fact, I wish it was just the two of us taking on this lot.'

The king nodded his approval. 'You know your places,' he said to the nobles. 'God be with you.'

As the English prepared to ride, the French herald, Montjoy, appeared once more, enquiring about Henry's ransom. 'Last chance,' he said, 'to save your poor men from certain massacre.'

The king was furious. 'Who sent you this time?' he demanded.

'The Constable of France.'

'Give him this message,' grated Henry. 'Say, your soldiers better catch me before they start wittering on about ransom. And tell him if our men die, their corpses'll send up such a stink, it'll spread a plague through all France.' He glared at Montjoy. 'Don't come again, Herald. There'll be no surrender, and no ransom.'

Montjoy bowed. 'I'll tell him, King Henry. And so fare thee well – thou never shalt hear herald any more.' His words held a suggestion of grudging admiration for this stubborn, doomed monarch.

The Duke of York begged the honour of leading the English charge. Henry granted his request and said, 'Now soldiers, march away; and how thou pleasest, God, dispose the day!'

Act Four

Charging knights, an awesome clatter make,
At whose approach, the stoutest heart may break.
Those steely, thund'rous hooves, those gleaming lances
Cause gallant men to set at nought their chances.
But hold: there lurks a simple twist of fate
As patiently, the English bowmen wait.

The French and English knights galloped their chargers at one another, and the battle began. The foot soldiers met and mingled, slashing and hacking. Blood spurted and fell, soaking the earth. The air was filled with the clash of steel on steel, the cries of men and the whickering squeals of terrified horses.

In some part of the battlefield, the rogue Pistol managed to get the better of a French soldier and went to take him prisoner. The boy was with him.

'Yield, cur!' he growled.

'You are, I think, the gentleman of good quality,' whined the Frenchman in his own language, eyeing Pistol's weapon.

'*Callity?*' hooted Pistol, who knew no French. 'Are you a hofficer or sommink? What's yer name, you Froggy git?'

'O, Seigneur Dieu!' said the frightened Frenchman.

'O, Seigneur Dieu's a gentleman, no danger,' asserted Pistol. 'Perpend my words, and mark: I'll skewer you and fink noffink of it, unless you coughs up an egregious ransom.'

'O, show mercy,' begged the prisoner. 'Have pity on me.'

(The French for me is *moi*; Pistol heard it as moy.)

'Moy?' he cried. 'Don't you moy *me*, sunshine. I wants forty moys, minimum, or I'll slit yer bleedin' froat.'

'Is it impossible,' wept the Frenchman, 'to escape the power of your arm?'

(Arm in French is *bras*.) '*Brass?*' yelled Pistol. 'You've the nerve to offer me brass, you foreign pillock?'

'O, *pardonnez-moi*,' said the prisoner.

'Wot the 'ell's *that* mean, eh? Ton of moys, is it?' He called the boy. ''Ere boy – ask him in French wot his name is.'

'*Ecoutez*,' said the boy to the Frenchman. '*Comment etes-vous appele?*'

'Monsieur le Fer.'

'He says his name is Master Fer.'

'Master Fer,' sneered Pistol. 'I'll fer 'im and firk 'im and ferret 'im – tell 'im that in French.'

The boy looked blank. 'I don't know the French for fer, ferret nor firk.'

'Well tell him to get ready, I'm gonna cut 'is froat.'

The prisoner was apprehensive. 'What's he saying?' he asked the boy in French.

The boy shrugged. 'He orders me to tell you to get ready, 'cos he's about to cut your throat.'

'Aye,' confirmed Pistol, 'I'll coopay votra gorge all right, unless you comes up wiv crowns and plenty of 'em, quick-sticks.'

'O, I beg you!' cried the Frenchman, 'for the

love of God, forgive me. I am the gentleman of a good house. Spare my life and I will give you two hundred crowns.'

'What's he rabbiting on about now?' asked Pistol, irritably.

'Says he's a gentleman, and if you'll spare his life he'll give you two hundred crowns.'

'Tell 'im,' instructed Pistol, 'that I'm not as mad wiv 'im as I was, and I'll take the crowns.'

'What does he say?' asked the Frenchman.

'He says, although it is against his oath to pardon any prisoner, nevertheless, for the crowns you have promised, he is happy to grant you liberty.'

'On my knees,' babbled the prisoner, 'I give a thousand thanks, and I guess happily that I fell into the hands of a knight, I think, most brave, valiant and very distinguished Lord of England.'

'What was all that, boy?' asked Pistol.

The boy told him what the Frenchman had said.

Pistol preened. 'I will show mercy,' he said. 'Follow me.'

'You're to follow the fine captain,' said the boy to the Frenchman. He watched the man hurry after the strutting rogue.

What a plonker that Pistol is, he thought. *Talk about empty vessels. Bardolph and Nym were braver than him, and they're both hanged. He'd be hanged, too, if he'd the guts to steal boldly instead of sneaking about. Think I'll go join the lackeys guarding the camp's baggage. Good job the French don't know there's only boys watching it.*

As the French cavalry thundered towards the English lines, Henry's bowmen snapped into action, loosing salvo after salvo of arrows into the air. So deftly did they shoot, nock and shoot again, the sky was never empty of shafts that soared, arced and dropped like a dense hailstorm among the French knights. Stricken horses reared, squealing. Men toppled from their saddles, pierced often by more than one arrow. The charge faltered, milled and broke up. There was no defence against the deadly hail of shafts. The proud mounted nobles of France were scattered without even having reached the rag-tag army they'd so lately mocked.

'O, diable!' swore the Constable of France.

'O, Lord,' cried Orleans. 'The day is lost – all is lost!

'God's *death*,' grated the dauphin. 'It's gone – *everything's* gone. We'll be a *joke*, folk'll laugh themselves sick.' A bugle sounded retreat. 'O, evil fortune, don't run away – don't!'

'Why not?' gasped the constable. 'They've broken our ranks, there's nothing we can do.'

'O, the *shame*,' moaned the dauphin. 'We'll have to kill ourselves. Are *these* the plonkers we laughed at?'

'Is their king the waster we were going to ransom?' asked Orleans bitterly.

Bourbon spoke to rally the nobles. 'Turn – turn and advance. Though all is lost, let's at least die facing the enemy.'

And so the remains of the French cavalry wheeled, charged and were cut down.

In another part of the field, King Henry, the Duke of Exeter and other nobles gathered, shepherding a flock of prisoners.

'You've fought bravely,' said the king, 'but it isn't over yet. Some of the French are still fighting.'

'The Duke of York has fallen, your Majesty,' said Exeter, 'and the Earl of Suffolk. They died comforting each other, and I cried to witness it.' He shook his head. 'My mother came into my eyes and gave me up to tears.'

'I don't blame you,' replied the king. 'I'm close to tears just hearing of it.'

A bugle sounded. The king looked round. 'What's this? The French have rallied their men and regrouped. Tell every soldier to kill his prisoners, lest they flee and rejoin the battle.'

As this grisly deed proceeded, Captains

Fluellen and Gower discovered another. Some French troops fleeing the battlefield had come upon the English luggage, killed the boys guarding it and plundered the king's tent.

'It's completely against the law of arms, look you,' cried Fluellen.

Gower nodded. 'The cowards haven't left one boy alive, and they've nicked the king's gear. No wonder he's ordered the prisoners killed.'

As the captain spoke, the king himself approached with Warwick, Gloucester, Exeter and other nobles. They had some prisoners with them.

'I was not angry since I came to France,' said Henry, 'till now.' He gazed at the mutilated corpses of the luggage boys, then turned to his friends. 'From this moment, we kill every Frenchman we find. We take no prisoners – flee or die are their only choices. Start with the prisoners here.'

'My liege, the herald of the French is here again,' said Exeter.

Gloucester looked at the dejected Montjoy. 'His eyes are humbler than they used to be,' he observed.

'Now then, Montjoy,' greeted Henry. 'Come about that ransom, have you?'

The herald shook his head. 'I seek permission to bury our dead,' he said.

'So soon?' queried the king. 'I don't even know yet who's won the day: there are still French horsemen galloping about the field.'

'The day is yours,' murmured Montjoy.

'God's doing then, not ours,' said Henry. 'Tell me, Herald, what's the name of that castle over there?'

'They call it Agincourt.'

'Then this will be known as the field of Agincourt, fought on Crispin's Day.'

Fluellen spoke up. 'Your Majesty's great-grandfather and great uncle, the Black Prince, fought a brave battle here in France, isn't it?'

'They did, Fluellen,' agreed the king.

'Yes, and Welsh soldiers played a gallant

part, see, fighting in a garden where leeks grew, wearing leeks in their caps, so that the leek has become an honourable badge of the service.' He smiled. 'In fact I think you wear the leek yourself on Saint David's Day.'

'I do,' confirmed Henry, 'for I'm Welsh myself, y'know.'

Fluellen strutted away, glowing with pride.

'Heralds,' commanded the king, 'go with my countryman, count the dead of both sides and let me have the tally.'

A soldier came by, whom the king recognised. It was Williams, who had challenged him last night while he was disguised.

'Bring that fellow to me,' he ordered Exeter.

'Soldier,' said Exeter, 'the king wants a word with you.'

The man approached.

'Why d'you have a glove in your cap?' asked Henry.

'Sire, I've vowed to fight its owner, if he's alive.'

'An Englishman?'

'A swaggering loudmouth, your Majesty. If he claims his glove I'm going to batter him. Or, if I see my glove in *his* cap, I'll knock it off, and the head with it.'

The king looked at him. 'See you keep your vow, when you meet the fellow.'

'I will, my liege,' said the soldier.

'Who's your captain?' asked Henry.

'Captain Gower, sire.'

When Williams had gone, Henry called Fluellen to him and gave him Williams's glove. 'This belongs to an enemy of mine,' he said. 'Wear it in your cap, and if somebody claims it, you'll know he's not a friend and I want you to apprehend him.'

'It'll be an honour, your Majesty,' said Fluellen.

'Oh, and send Captain Gower to me.'

When the Welshman departed, Henry explained to Warwick and Gloucester what he'd done, and asked them to keep an eye on Fluellen. 'That glove might earn him a thick ear,' he chuckled. 'It belongs to a short-tempered soldier, and I wouldn't put it past Fluellen to overreact. Watch, and see nobody's seriously hurt.'

Presently, Captain Gower approached. As luck would have it, Williams was with him. 'I believe the king means to knight you, Captain,' he murmured.

At that moment, Fluellen also appeared. Williams saw his glove in the Welshman's cap.

'That's my glove!' Williams cried. 'So it was *you* last night, strutting and blowing. Take *that*!' He hit Fluellen hard across the face with Henry's glove.

'If this is your glove,' roared Fluellen, 'then you're the king's enemy and a damned traitor, and I'll arrest you if I don't kill you first.'

Warwick and Gloucester hurried forward. 'What's wrong?' asked Warwick.

'My lord of Warwick,' gasped Fluellen, 'it's treason – this man's an enemy of the king;

and here is the king.'

Henry approached. 'What is happening?'

'My liege,' gasped Fluellen, 'this man's a traitor and an enemy. He recognised the glove you gave me and struck me.'

'It's *my* glove,' protested Williams. 'Look – here's the match. I gave it to the puffed-up braggart I met last night, and vowed to batter him if I saw it in his cap.' He pointed to Fluellen. 'This is he, and I've kept my vow.'

'He's lying, your Majesty,' cried the Welshman. 'He's nothing but a low-down traitor. *You* gave me this glove – *tell* him.'

'Give me your glove, soldier,' commanded the king. 'See – here's the match, which you gave to me. It was *I* you vowed to strike.'

'But...' Williams shook his head. 'You didn't look like... You were disguised. I would never do anything to offend my king, your Majesty. Not knowingly. I can only beg you to pardon me.'

The king handed the soldier's glove to Exeter.

'Fill this with crowns,' he said, 'and give it to him.' He looked at Williams. 'Keep it, soldier, and wear it for an honour in your cap.'

A herald now approached. Henry turned to him. 'Are the dead counted?'

'Yes, my liege. This paper gives the tally of French dead.' He gave the king the slip of paper. Henry looked at Exeter. 'Which French nobles have we as prisoners, Uncle?'

'Charles, Duke of Orleans,' said Exeter. 'John, Duke of Bourbon and Lord Bouciqualt. Also fifteen hundred other lords and barons, knights and squires. And that's not counting the common men.'

Henry shook his head in amazement. 'This note says the French lost ten thousand men, of whom only sixteen hundred were peasants. That means they've lost eight thousand four hundred princes, barons, lords, knights, squires and gentlemen of blood and quality. It's beyond belief.' He looked at the herald. 'Do you have the tally of our English dead?'

'Right here, your Majesty.' He handed the king another paper.

'Edward Duke of York, the Earl of Suffolk, Sir Richard Kikely, Davy Gam Esquire.' Henry looked up. 'No others by name, and only twenty-five common soldiers.'

The difference in numbers of the French and English dead made Henry's victory even more stunning than it had seemed before. He was elated, but declined to claim any credit for himself. God, he said, had brought about this miraculous outcome.

Act Five

Imagine now the aftermath of battle:
The ruined grains and vines, the wasted cattle
All through France. And see how Henry and his bride
Spread healing peace across the countryside.
So may all warring men lay down their blades,
And wander arm in arm through sunlit glades.

Cheering crowds thronged the sands and quaysides as Henry's victorious army returned to England. More crowds lined the king's route from the coast to London. At Blackheath, Henry's lords urged him to display his bent sword and battered helmet before the ecstatic citizens, but he declined on grounds of modesty – the triumph at Agincourt had not been his own, but God's.

Everywhere they went, the king's soldiers were acclaimed as conquering heroes. As Henry had predicted on the eve of battle, thousands of men regretted not having been at Agincourt, and having no claim to a share in the glory.

As for the king, soon enough he was obliged to set sail again for France, to negotiate a settlement with the French king and his court.

At the English camp in France, Fluellen and Gower were having a conversation about the Welshman's favourite topic – leeks.

'Why are you wearing your leek today, Fluellen?' asked Gower. 'Saint David's Day is past.'

'I'm wearing it today,' replied Fluellen, 'because yesterday I meets that criminal waste of space, Pistol, and he's got bread and salt with him, see? And he tells me to eat my leek. *Eat your leek, boyo*, he says. And this is at a place where I can't kick his backside for him, nor twist his ear off, so I'm wearing my leek till we meets at a suitable spot, and there we'll see who eats what, isn't it?'

As the Welshman spoke, Pistol came into view.

'Talk of the devil,' cried Gower. 'And here he comes, swelling like a turkey-cock.'

Fluellen snorted. 'I doesn't give a stuff for his swellings, nor his turkey-cocks, neither. God bless you, Pistol, you scurvy, lousy knave – God bless you.'

'Looking for bovver are you, you Welsh git?' enquired Pistol. 'Bring it on if you fink you're hard enough, or else get lost – stink of leeks makes me want to puke.'

Fluellen plucked the leek from his cap. 'Makes you want to puke, isn't it? Then look you, I'm going to make you eat it.'

Pistol shook his head. 'No way, sunshine.'

Fluellen gave the villain a slap. 'Now will you eat?'

'You're *dead*, Welshman,' hissed Pistol. 'You're toast.'

'I'll be dead one day,' agreed Fluellen, 'as will we all. Meanwhile, here's your dinner, and *here's* a sauce to improve your appetite.' He punched Pistol in the mouth.

'That's enough,' growled Gower. 'You've made your point, Fluellen.'

'No.' The Welshman shook his head. 'He'll eat the leek, or I'll know the reason why.' He advanced on Pistol. 'Going to eat it, are you, or d'you want more sauce to help it down?'

Pistol was a coward, the sauce was not to his liking. He started to nibble the leek, and Fluellen stood over him till he'd eaten every shred.

'I'll have my revenge,' he vowed.

Gower shook his head. 'No, you won't, Pistol, you're all wind and wee-wee. But next time you hear a Welsh accent, you might not be quite so quick with the put-downs.'

Pistol slunk away with his onion breath, to resume his career as a sneak thief, and to claim that the bruises he'd had from Fluellen were wounds received at Agincourt.

As Pistol departed the English camp, King Henry and his nobles arrived at the palace of the King of France. Henry spoke cordial greetings to the king and queen, the king's sister

Katherine and the French nobles.

'We are happy to see your face, brother England,' said the king, 'and your entourage is most welcome also.'

The queen nodded agreement. 'May this meeting have a peaceful outcome,' she said. 'May your Majesty's eyes, lately filled with such hostility towards our people, look on us now with love.'

'We're here to say amen to that,' said Henry.

The Duke of Burgundy looked at both kings. 'It was no easy task for me,' he said, 'to bring the two of you together like this, face to face. I hope that now we can begin to move on, so that the long untended fields of France might be set in order, her ravaged crops replanted, her tangled vines pruned and her neglected meadows scythed. In short, it is my hope that peace might prevail, so that the young men of France may give up soldiering and relearn the skills that once kept our land productive.'

King Henry looked at the speaker. 'If you

want this peace, Duke of Burgundy, you must buy it by meeting all our demands, as set out in the paper you have been given.'

Burgundy nodded. 'The king's aware of your demands, but hasn't decided yet.'

'Well then,' retorted Henry, 'the peace you wish for is in his hands.'

'I've only skimmed them,' said the French king. 'I need to discuss them point by point with your representatives before I respond.'

'Fine,' agreed Henry. 'My uncle Exeter, together with Clarence, Gloucester, Warwick and Huntingdon will go over our demands with you.' He turned to the French queen. 'Will you go, too?'

Queen Isabella nodded. 'It might be as well that a woman's eye look things over.'

'Leave my cousin Katherine here with me,' said Henry. 'She's number one on my wish list.'

'She has my permission to stay,' said Isabella coolly, turning to follow her husband out of the room.

King Henry was now alone with Princess Katherine and Alice, her maid. He smiled at the princess. 'Will you teach this rough soldier some words of love, so that he may have the chance to win your heart?'

Katherine pouted. 'You are laughing at me, for the England I cannot speak.'

'Just tell me you like me,' pleaded Henry, 'and I won't care how the words come out.'

'What this means – *like me*?' asked the princess.

'An angel is like you, Katherine,' smiled the king, 'and you are like an angel.'

Katherine frowned. '*Que dit-il*? That I is like the *angel*?'

The maid nodded. '*Oui*, that is what he said.'

'I said it,' confirmed Henry, 'and I meant it.'

'*O, bon Dieu!*' gasped the princess, '*les langues des hommes sont pleines de tromperies.*'

The king looked at Alice. 'Did she just say men talk a lot of crap?'

The maid nodded. '*Oui* – that the mans talks

deceit. I don't know what is crap.'

Henry laughed. 'She speaks English better than I do.' He gazed at Katherine. 'Oh look – just tell me you understand that I love you, and say you love me. If you ask more French of me than that, you'll think yourself courted by a clodhopper who sold his farm and bought a crown.'

The princess nodded. 'I understand, but...'

'What?'

'Is it possible for me to love the enemy of France?'

The king shook his head. 'No, Kate, it is not possible for you to love the enemy of France, but in loving me you will love the *friend* of France.' He smiled. 'I love France so much, I will not part with a village of it; I will have it all mine. And Kate, when France is mine and I am yours, then yours is France and you are mine.'

The Princess looked bewildered. 'I ... cannot this follow.'

Henry pulled a face. 'I suppose I'd better

try it in French then, God help us both. Er ...
*Je quand sur le possession de France, et quand vous
avez le possession de moi* .... uh, *donc votre est
France et vous etes mienne.*' He shook his head
and sighed. 'I'm never going to move you in
French, Kate, except to laugh at me.'

Katherine shrugged. 'Your French is as good
as my English, I think.'

'You may be right,' conceded Henry, 'but do
you love me?'

'This I cannot tell,' murmured the princess.

'Well, look,' suggested Henry, 'when you're
alone with Alice in your chamber, ask her what
she thinks of me. Ask your friends, too, and
your family.' He smiled. 'For myself, I can't
help believing that with the help of Saint Denis
and Saint George, you and I will produce a
warrior son, half French, half English, who will
one day march on Constantinople and sieze the
Turk by the beard.'

The pair continued to joust with lances of
broken language till the French king returned

with the English lords. He had agreed to all of Henry's demands, including Princess Katherine's hand in marriage.

'Take her, fair son,' he said, 'and from her blood raise up issue to me; that the contending kingdoms of France and England may cease their hatred; and never war advance his bleeding sword 'twixt England and fair France.'

'Amen to that,' intoned the assembled lords, and Henry, King of England and of France, sealed the pact with a kiss on the lips of his future Queen.

About the Author

The play contains some of the most familiar lines in the English language. What Briton does not recognise these words, spoken by King Henry before the battle of Harfleur:

Once more unto the breach, dear friends, once more; or close the wall up with our English dead.

Or these, on the field of Agincourt:

We few, we happy few, we band of brothers. … gentlemen in England now abed shall think themselves accursed they were not here, and hold thier manhood cheap while any speaks that fought with us upon Saint Crispin's Day.

'Marvellous stuff,' my English tutor at college used to say. I couldn't see it then, not really, but then I wasn't a writer, hadn't known the frustration of searching for exactly the right words with which to express a complex emotion, and falling short every time. Every time.

Will Shakespeare never fell short. That was his genius, and that's why his words have resonated across the centuries, and will continue to do so.

It's why my name sharing a page with his is more honour than I could possibly earn.